YOU FOR ME

DOWN TO RIDE FOR HIS HOOD LOVE

UNIQUE

1

———

BRISCOE

"Y'all done made it to the airport yet?" I asked with my eyes glued to the road as I maneuvered through my hood.

"Yeah... I just pulled up."

"Selah fly in with them?"

"To my knowledge, she did."

"Where you putting everybody at?" I asked.

Rae let out an aggravated sigh. "My parents gon' have to coexist for the week because I don't have anywhere else to put them."

I proposed to Rae at our baby shower, and after two years, we were finally getting married. When the baby was born, all of our time and attention went to her, so the wedding got pushed back.

"You know Veronica gon' be pissed off about that."

"I know. I know. But I can't put them in the house. Everybody else staying with us."

"I'on know, Rae baby. I'on think that shit gon' go well."

"It was your idea to invite my dad's wife, not mine."

"It didn't make sense for yo' pops to be here and not extend the invite to his wife."

When we found Rae was pregnant, I made her have a sit-down with her folks. I grew up with just my mom and Granny G, and I didn't want that for my kid. The issues that they had didn't have shit to do with Rae and Selah, but somehow, it caused the whole family to be at a divide. When they sat down and got everything out on the table, her relationship with each of them improved.

The closer it got to Rae's due date, she wanted her dukes there for the delivery, and she never went home, so she'd been living in our guest house for the past two years. Rae took an extended leave of absence from her job to stay at home 'cause I refused to put my baby in daycare. Both of Rae's parents played an active role in Saje's life, but we tried to keep them out of each other's presence. Rae's ass done decided to put Raemon—her daddy—in the house with her dukes when she knew that shit wasn't gon' work out right.

"But you know how my mama is."

"Yeah, I do... which is why I thought you had a plan in place. But it is what it is. We gon' have to rock with it. Where my baby at?"

"She back at the house with Ma."

"I'm 'bout to pull up on Kayo. You and Saje wanna meet me for lunch?"

"Yeah. We can do that. Just let me know when you're on the way."

"Bet... but aye, don't let it stress you out. We're days from the wedding. Everything is going to be okay."

"I believe you."

"Good. I love you."

"I love you too," she promised before we ended the call.

Getting out of the truck, I slid my phone in the pocket of my shorts before hitting the lock. My cousin, Kayo, was throwing a party on the block, and I promised him that I would pull up on him. I didn't have plans on staying long, which was why I'd invited Rae to lunch. I walked through the house and spoke to everybody before making my way out to the backyard. I spotted Kayo kneeled down in a circle shooting dice.

"There the king of Miami go right there," Kayo boasted when he stood up to shake my hand.

"Fuck ya, my boy."

"You gon' get in on this action?" he asked.

"Y'all niggas don't want me to get in on that."

"You done been in Atlanta so long yo' ass done forgot how to shoot dice." He joked. Kayo and every nigga in the hood swore I wasn't the same nigga I was before I moved to Atlanta. I'd been kicking it in the streets my whole life. That shit wasn't on me; it was in me. Unlike them, I had other things to live for. I couldn't stand on the corner and hustle my whole life. I liked to kick back and let my money come to me. Most of the niggas that I grew up hustling with were still in the same spot hustling backward. I probably would've been too if Red and I hadn't linked up with that nigga Priest.

"I might've been raised in Hollywood, but I ain't never been Hollywood," I said with a shrug.

"Aye, Selah coming down for the wedding?"

"Nigga, that's her sister. Of course she coming down. And no, you still can't holla at her."

"Boy stay cockblocking."

I snatched the dice from his hand. "Nigga, you heard what I said. But fuck all of that. Now you gotta see me." Shaking the dice in my palm, I blew on them before tossing them on the ground. When they rolled to a stop, the niggas standing in the circle hollered. "Yep... Run me them pockets, nigga. This 'bout to be an easy come up."

———

After taking all them niggas' money, I hopped in the truck and drove down the block to G's crib. Everybody in the hood knew what kind of truck I pushed, so if she caught wind of me being there without pushing up on here, I would never hear the end of it. I could hear G's loud mouth from outside on the porch. I tapped on the screen door a couple of times before pulling it open and entering the house.

"Granny G," I called out when I stepped into the living room where she was.

"Um-hmm, I was waiting on you to show up. Martha had already called me and told me you was down by Kayo." Leaning over, I pecked her on the forehead before sitting back on the couch.

"You knew I was gon' stop by and see you."

"That's what your mouth say... You ready for the wedding? You ain't nervous, is you?"

"Nervous for what, G? Me and Rae been engaged for a lil' minute. Marriage is the obvious next step."

"I don't know, Scoota. You could be nervous and having second thoughts."

"Nawl, G. I'm solid in my decision. Rae and Saje the best thing that done happened to me in a lil' minute," I admitted.

"Why you ain't bring my baby down here with you?" she queried.

Granny G and Rae might not always see eye to eye, but Saje was definitely G's baby. Rae never let their issues keep G from having a relationship with Saje. If anything, she made me bring Saje to visit her a lot 'cause she knew she was lonely. G lived alone in the hood, and I'd tried several times to put her up in a better neighborhood, but she didn't wanna leave her crib.

"Rae went to pick her family up from the airport, so she left the baby at home with her dukes."

"Oh... That's cute."

"Don't start, G. I need you on your best behavior for the wedding."

"I know how to act, boy… Kacen said him and Angel gon' bring the baby by when they make it."

"Yeah, I talked to him this morning. They're leaving out later."

Before Angel had the baby, Red bought a house out this way. They frequented Miami so everybody could spend time with baby Saint. Netta and Rae had been trying to talk them into moving out here, but Angel didn't wanna leave her job.

"Scoota, you protecting your assets?" G queried.

"What you mean, G?"

"Hear me out… I know when people get married, they're thinking about forever. But with the way you young folks bounce from bed to bed, you gotta plan for anything. You got all of these rental properties and trying to buy these apartment buildings. You stand to lose a lot if you and Rae was to ever get a divorce."

"What you trying to say, G?"

"You making Rae sign a prenup?"

I shook my head. "Nawl, G… Me and Rae locked in for a lifetime, and even if we wasn't, she got my seed, so she can get anything she want."

"Divorce is messy, Scoota, and it brings out the worst in folks. Protect yourself and your investments. Get an attorney to put in writing what she gets in case y'all ever split. I know you gon' take care of Saje, but you ain't gotta take care of her mama if y'all ain't together."

"Rae ain't that type of person, G, and you know that. If I bring up the idea of a prenup, ain't gone be no wedding."

"At the end of the day, Rae is still a woman. Women can be vindictive. You best protect yourself. If she has an issue signing a prenup, that should let you know what type of woman she is."

G had just fucked my head up. If Rae and I decided to separate, I would take care of her no doubt. Did I think she would purposely try and take what I'd built? Nawl. But thinking about it from all ends, a prenup would protect not only me but her as well. Rae had her own bag and definitely didn't need me or my money.

Along with the rental properties I had, I was in the process of trying to purchase run-down apartment complexes in the hood. I was gon' hire a team to renovate them and turn them into luxury apartments that were affordable for low-income families. I was putting my blood, sweat, and tears into building my hood back up. The last thing I needed was somebody snatching that shit from under me.

Running my hand over my dreads, I let out a sigh. "I'ma come at her head about it, but I can already see where the conversation is going to go."

"Talk it over with your lawyer and watch him tell you that I'm right."

Pulling out my phone, I texted Rae a location for lunch

and stood to leave. "I believe you, G. I'ma get up out of here. I'm 'bout to go meet Rae and the baby on Ocean for lunch."

"Alright, Scoota. Bring Saje by here tomorrow."

I walked out of G's crib and made a mental note to call Boss and talk to him about the whole prenup thing. I had to figure out a way to bring the idea up to Rae without letting her know that G was the one who orchestrated the whole idea. I was praying that shit didn't come back to bite me in the ass.

WHEN I PULLED up to the Sugar Factory, Rae and the baby were already seated. Saje was sitting on the table in front of Rae when I walked up. When her eyes landed on me, she smiled and yelled out for me.

"Daddy," she squealed.

"Sajeee..." I sang in response as I pulled her up from the table. I blew into her cheeks while she laughed and tried to wiggle out of my arms. "Saje, I missed you, baby."

"Saje the only one you missed?" Rae sassed.

Leaning down, I pecked her lips several times. "Nawl. I missed you too, Rae baby."

"Yeah, nigga. That's what I thought," she added.

Taking the seat across from her, I adjusted Saje in my lap and stared at Rae. She had on a pair of denim cut-off shorts, a white body suit, and the white and pink Louis Vuitton sneakers I bought her. She had her long braids thrown up in a bun in the top of her head.

"Why you looking at me like that?" she quizzed.

"Looking at you like what?"

"I'on know... Like that."

"I'm looking at you 'cause you looking good to a nigga, that's all."

Rae blushed and rolled her eyes. "Okay, sir."

"You got everybody settled?"

"Yeah... My mama acted a damn fool when my dad nem walked into the house. I'm sure if she ain't have the baby in her arms, she would've swung on one of them."

"As long as they keep that shit back there and away from my baby, they can box it out all night."

"How many days we got until the wedding?"

"Six."

She massaged her temples, sighing dejectedly. "Why does it feel so far away?"

"'Cause you're stressing over the lil' shit. Everything gon' be good. You talk to the girls?" I asked, trying to change the subject. I knew Rae would be on edge until her girls got there. For the first time in a long time, neither of them was pregnant, so I knew they had plans to show their asses this week.

"Yeah. They leaving tonight when Mielle get off. Red and Angel will be here tomorrow at noon. Saint gotta get his shots before they leave."

"Bet..." I said and picked up the menu to look over it before signaling for the waitress. After placing our orders, we went over last-minute wedding details while we waited for the food.

———

I intently watched Rae as she rubbed Saje's back and kissed the top of her head. Halfway through lunch, my baby got full and decided that she was ready for a nap.

We had finished eating. I had purposely gotten Rae a few shots so she could be calm. I knew she wouldn't show out in public, but I needed her to be relaxed before I brought up the idea of a prenup.

"Rae baby... I need to run something by you, listen to what I'm saying before you react."

"Oh Lord. What's wrong?"

"Ain't nothing wrong. But what do you think about us getting a prenup?"

She stopped rocking and gazed at me. After a few seconds, she spoke up. "I don't know... Is this your way of telling me that you want one?"

"I've been thinking..." *Lie number one.* "A nigga would like to believe that everything lasts forever, but the reality is, sometimes shit happens that we don't plan for. In the event that we don't make it, a prenup would ensure that we're both protected."

"Why wait until the week of the wedding to bring it up?"

"Honestly, I just thought about it. We're both going into this marriage with assets that we acquired before we got together. I think it'll be smart to keep those separated from the ones that we gain while married."

"If we were to get a divorce, I wouldn't want anything from you but for you to do your part when it comes to Saje."

"I know that... But we could sit down with Boss and discuss the terms, and once we've reached an agreement, we can sign off on it, making things legal. That would guarantee a clean-cut split, and we wouldn't have to spend unnecessary money in court trying to divide anything up."

"I get it, but it makes me leery because what if we do sign one and down the line my personal finances change. I mean, like right now, I've been off work since I had Saje. Being that you pay all of the bills at the house and take care of everything else, I haven't had to spend my money. Though I'm not solely dependent on you, you are the primary bread winner. I wouldn't want Saje to grow up accustomed to living one way and something happens where I can't continue to provide that."

"I understand everything that you're saying. That's why I said we can sit down with Boss when he gets in town and discuss what you would want and what I'm willing to give."

"Willing to give?" she repeated with her head cocked to the side.

"Not like that, Rae. I'm just saying we would have to really decide what we would want and what we're comfortable with parting with."

"I don't know if I like this. It feels like you have no faith that we will last," she mumbled with uncertainty.

"Me either, baby, and I do have faith in us. But unfortunately, this is one of those things that we have to discuss before we walk down the aisle. I'm sorry for bringing it up days before the wedding, but I've been so focused on trying to give you the wedding of your dreams that it slipped my mind. Now that we're in the home stretch, we got some logistics to figure out."

"When will Boss be here?"

"He flying in Thursday. I can call him up beforehand about it, or we can set up a time to have him come by so we could talk."

"And this prenup was your idea? You ain't let nobody put the thought in your head, did you?"

"So you trying to say that a nigga can't think for himself?" I huffed offensively.

In that moment, I could've told Rae that the idea came from G, but she would've taken it the wrong way. Since the beginning, G felt like Rae was with me for the wrong reasons. I'd never thought that 'cause I had to damn near beg her ass to leave Atlanta and move to Miami. If that shit with Cream hadn't have happened when it did, she probably would've held off. When we moved, I made sure to put her name on the house to give her a sense of security. I made a promise to her that I would always make sure that she was good. Prenup or not, I would always stick to my word.

Rae threw her hands up in surrender. "I'm just double checking."

"Nawl... This one on me, Rae."

She eyed me suspiciously before conceding. "Okay... Well, when Boss gets here, we can sit down and talk about it. I'm open to it as long as you promise that we're going to be okay."

Reaching across the table, I grabbed one of her hands and stared into her eyes. "You for me, Rae."

When we left the Sugar Factory, I didn't feel no more at ease than I did before I got there. I had this nagging feeling that the whole thing was gon' blow up in my face. I prayed that Boss would be able to give Rae the clarity that I couldn't provide. I followed her back to the crib with the weight of the world on my shoulders.

2

RAE

"That looks good on you, Angel," I said as I studied the way the dress clung to her tiny frame. We were at Lovely Bride Miami doing the last fitting. For the girls, I selected a red, halter-neck, fishtail dress. Angel had been insecure about her body after giving birth to Saint, so she was worried about the way she would look in the dress.

"Thank you. I was praying that it worked out since Kacen wouldn't let me get any lipo done," she replied as she looked herself over in the mirror.

"Bitch, what you gone lipo," I retorted.

"My midsection," she said and pointed to her stomach.

"Girl, Saint filled yo' ass out. You look really good," Mielle admitted.

"And you snapped back fast as hell," Suny added.

"This is the heaviest that I've ever been, and it makes me a little insecure at times."

"I'm sure your husband doesn't feel the same," my mama said as she plopped down on the couch beside me.

"No, Ms. Veronica. Kacen loves it."

"Then yo' ass should too," Ma Dukes replied.

Angel stepped off the pedestal and walked back into the fitting room. I watched my mama out the corner of my eye downing her fourth glass of champagne.

"Don't get too lit, girl, 'cause you gon' have Saje tonight while we go out."

"Let your daddy and his wife watch her. I'm trying to go see a friend."

My face scrunched up involuntarily. "What friend?"

"That's for me to know and you to wonder about," she bragged, causing my sister scoff and roll her eyes.

"How you feeling, Rae?" Suny asked.

"Ready for it to be over with. We've been planning for months, and the time is finally here."

"You been stressing?" Mielle queried.

"Not really stressing... It's the checking behind people that I've hired to do a job that I don't like."

"Yeah... I understand that. It's your special day, so you're more anal about it than they are. We're five days away though. I'm ready for this bachelorette party."

"Me too," the other girls voiced agreeing with Mielle.

"I got a question… Did either of you sign a prenuptial agreement?"

"Prenup? Bitch, I wish Priest would've asked me for a damn prenup. We wouldn't be married right now."

"Me and Kacen got married on a whim. We didn't have time for a prenup."

"Kross and I don't have one either. Why?"

Hearing all of them admit to not having a prenup really made me feel some type of way. I kept telling myself that Briscoe wasn't being shady as fuck for asking me to sign one. But something about the situation wasn't sitting right.

"When we were at lunch yesterday, Briscoe brought it up in conversation."

"That nigga asked you to sign a prenup?" Ma Dukes bellowed.

"We talked about it," I admitted.

"How did it make you feel?" Angel asked.

"Honestly, I don't know how to feel. I feel like when people sign prenups, they already have this preconceived notion that the marriage isn't forever. Had he asked in the beginning, I probably would feel more comfortable with it, but he asked me six days before we're set to walk down the aisle."

"I don't think he has malicious intent, Rae. Briscoe loves you," Selah argued.

"Love or not, the nigga asked her for a prenup. What he think? You supposed to walk away with nothing?"

"The way he was talking, that's not what he meant at all, Ma. I know he gon' always take care of Saje, but what if we divorce and I fall on hard times? Don't get me wrong, I can make some shit shake, but I'm pushing forty. The last thing I'm about to do is jump back on stage and start shaking my ass." I rubbed my temples and sighed. "I don't know, y'all. It definitely made me feel some type of way."

"Did you express your concerns to him?"

"Suny, everything that I'm saying to y'all, I said to him." Feeling myself get emotional, I dropped my head into my hands. "It's not even about the money 'cause I don't want anything from him. I feel like even if he say he don't, a part of him feels like I'm with him for what he can do for me. God knows Granny G been saying I was a sack chaser since the beginning."

"Briscoe knows the type of person you are, Rae. Maybe it is for protection. Granted, I don't know why he would need protection. Didn't y'all go through premarital counseling?"

"Yep... Our last session was this past Saturday."

"And this didn't come up then?"

I shook my head. "Not once during the six weeks, which is another reason I'm like *what the fuck*. 'Cause where it just pop up from?"

"I don't know, Rae," Suny muttered.

"Me either. But if I don't sign one, does that mean we won't get married?"

"Nonsense, girl. Y'all still getting married. Just reach out to your attorney and let them negotiate your terms," Angel said.

"We're supposed to sit down with Boss when he comes on Thursday. Who, by the way, is each of our attorney."

"Then you may need to retain another one for this situation. Antron is both mine and Priest's attorney too, and he's definitely not biased, but if it makes you feel better, then reach out to someone else."

"Thank, y'all... I got two days to figure it out. I'll have a plan in place by then."

"Don't wait too late, Raegan. I know how you are."

"I won't, Mama. I promise."

Truth was I didn't know what kind of plan I was going to come up with. I didn't have too much time to ponder over it, 'cause tonight was the night that both families would come face-to-face for the first time in a couple of years. The last time being my baby shower. Ma Dukes had been living with us since I'd given birth. She and Netta got along good, but she held the same disdain for Granny G that I did, so they weren't around each other often. Briscoe had rented out Prime 112 for the event, and I couldn't wait to see everyone.

***

BRISCOE and I were fashionably late for dinner. Saje wouldn't cooperate for shit tonight. She cried the entire time I was getting her dressed. I almost cancelled on dinner to stay in with her, but her daddy wouldn't let that happen. Briscoe had that girl so spoiled he lay in the recliner with her until she stopped fussing long enough for me to get myself together. He was such a hands-on dad, and I appreciated him for that. She wouldn't let him strap her into the car seat, so I drove us to the restaurant while he held her in his lap.

When we pulled up to the restaurant, I handed valet the key and walked around to the passenger's side. I held my arms out for Saje, but she turned her head and grabbed ahold to her daddy's shirt.

"Saje, you being real extra tonight."

"Leave my baby alone, Rae. She probably tired. Yo' pops nem had her out at the beach all day."

"Nawl, her lil' ass just bossy." I rolled my eyes and walked off.

When we walked into the restaurant,, everyone stopped what they were doing and cheered. I smiled and did a quick shimmy before taking my place at the table. Briscoe took Saje over to where Granny G and Netta was sitting so they could see her. I noticed that she started whining when Granny G held her arms out for her.

After talking with his family, he came and sat down beside me. I purposely had the restaurant to sit us at the table with our friends. I loved my family, but I could only tolerate them in moderation. Since Saje didn't wanna deal with me, I reached for Saint, who gladly came. When I had him secured in my arms, I looked at Saje and stuck my tongue out at her.

"Kayo, what I tell you 'bout that?" Briscoe's voiced boomed beside me. When I looked over to the right, I noticed that his cousin Kayo had his arm wrapped around the back of my sister's chair.

"Kinfolk, I'm just talking to her," he said, smiling, showcasing his mouth full of golds.

"Better keep Kayo away from Selah. My daddy gon' kill his ass," I whispered.

"I told him the other day to leave her alone. Nigga don't damn listen." I laughed. Briscoe was overprotective of Selah just like he was Saje. So he meant business when he told Kayo he couldn't fuck with her. His ass was too old for her anyway.

"When we put the baby down tonight, you gon' let me hit you with that pressure?"

"You better hit me with something, or I'ma be one mad bitch. You flaked on me last night."

"Nigga was tired, Rae. I'ma make that shit up to you when we get home."

"You better, and don't be trying to stay up all night smoking with Priest ass or you gon' be sleeping in the room with him and Mielle."

"Yeah, whatever you say."

The servers went around passing out drinks and appetizers while everyone at the table chatted amongst themselves. To keep from having to wait on everybody to order, I'd preselected the menu for tonight. So far, everyone seemed to be getting along really well. Hopefully, it stayed that way.

———

Once dinner was over, we walked around the room and mingled with our guests. I introduced him to some of my family that he hadn't met. It was the first time that a lot of my family was meeting Saje as well. I ended up at the table with my dad and his wife casually chatting about nothing. I didn't miss the daggers that my mom was shooting my way the whole time my dad's wife, Kim, played with Saje.

"Raegan, Selah told me that she decided to move down here with you and Ron."

"Yeah, Dad... I've been trying for a while. Since Ma is going to be moving out of the guest house soon, Selah's going to stay there until she finds a place of her own."

"Your moms moving away from y'all?"

"Briscoe has a rental property in Coral Gables that she's moving into."

"Oh okay... That's nice of him to let her move there."

"It was... She's been a big help with the baby, and I plan on going back to work after the honeymoon, so I need her here."

"Sounds like y'all got it planned out," Kim said.

"Yeah... It's been a long time coming. I've been working

since my freshman year in college. It was cool to sit out and be at home, but I've never been the type to sit on my hands. If there's a bag, I guarantee you I'm out there chasing it."

"Rae baby..." Briscoe called my name. He was sitting at the table with Granny G and his mom. I held my hand up and focused my attention on Saje.

"Y'all gon' be okay with her while I go and see what he wants?"

"Go ahead, Rae. I got my grandbaby," my dad asserted. Getting up from the table, I went to where Briscoe was.

"Yes, love?" He scooted his chair back from the table and patted his lap for me to sit down.

"G wanna know if you having strippers at your bachelorette party."

I didn't know if this shit was a setup or not. Briscoe was adamant about me not having male strippers at my bachelorette party, but Mielle had booked the dancer Bolo, along with some females from King of Diamonds.

"I'm having female dancers, not any men."

"Ah shit. I thought I was gon' see some dick slanging."

"My dick the only one Rae gon' be watching slang," Briscoe said as he wrapped his arms around my waist.

"You coming to the party, G?"

"I'on wanna see no naked ass unless it's on a man," she fussed.

"If you wanna come, I'm sure I can find somebody for you." Granny G was hot and cold. When she wanted to be nice to me, she was. I had never did shit to her old ass, so I took what I could get. If she wanted to come out and party, then I would definitely allow her to. Maybe a night of fun would help her remove that stick she had up her ass.

"What I tell you, Rae?" Briscoe asked.

"It ain't for me though... G wanna see some men."

"G ain't going nowhere either but to the damn house."

"Scoota, you ain't the boss of me. Rae, get me a big fine one, and I'll make sure to bring my ones."

"Yeah, aite," Briscoe mumbled into my back.

"Netta, where my mama went?" I asked, looking around the restaurant to see if I could spot her.

"She took a phone call outside." I nodded my head and listened to G and Briscoe fuss about her wanting to see a stripper.

Before long, Red and Angel were joining us at the table. Granny G took Saint out of Red's arms and kissed all over his cheeks.

"Granny G, you gon' have my boy spoiled if you don't stop."

"Oh, hush up, Kacen. This boy ain't gon' be no more spoiled than you were. I hope y'all got him a good bag packed 'cause I'm taking him home with me when we leave."

"I knew you were, so I made sure to pack extra," Angel said. Unlike Briscoe, Red didn't mind Saint spending the night with someone else. Briscoe's number-one rule was that we slept in the house together every single night unless he had to go out of town for business and we didn't go with him. That was another reason my mama never left Miami. If it weren't for the fact that she stayed with us, she would only see the baby every few months when we came to town.

"When Veronica moving in, Rae?" Netta asked.

"It was supposed to be this past weekend, but she decided to wait until after we get back from the honeymoon."

"Where she moving to?" Granny G queried.

"The house in Coral Gables," Briscoe shared as he ran his hands up and down my thigh.

Granny G squinted her eyes and looked at Briscoe. "What house in Coral Gables?"

"The house you ain't want, G," Red said.

"What you mean house she ain't want?" I asked. 'Cause I didn't know he had bought the house for G. Had I known, I would've told him to put my mama somewhere else. I didn't want no unnecessary issues with G.

"The house yo' dukes moving into is the one I bought and fixed up with G in mind. She ain't want it, so when you mentioned that Veronica wanted to her own spot, I suggested that one. It's closer to your job and not too far from the crib."

"Mama, you can't get mad, 'cause he offered it to you, and you said it was too far from everybody," Nettta added.

"Hush up, Netta... Ain't nobody mad. I was just wondering. *One.*"

Briscoe kissed me on my exposed shoulder, trying to butter me up. "Anyway, in the morning, I want y'all to come over so we can have breakfast. It's just for immediate family, something more private and intimate for us to do before the festivities began."

"You cooking, Rae?" Netta asked.

"Nawl, her ass ain't cooking. She made me hire a chef."

"Shut up, Briscoe. Chef Baul came highly recommended."

"That's nice, Scoota," Granny G expressed. "*Two.*"

"G, you going senile or something?" Red probed, rubbing his hand across her forehead.

"Senile?" Briscoe repeated and looked between the two of them.

"Y'all ain't hear her over here counting?"

"I heard it..." I admitted.

"Ain't nobody going senile, Kacen. And ain't nobody heard me counting nothing 'cause I ain't said nothing." I looked at Red, and he looked at me. I wasn't going crazy. I clearly heard G say one and two. I looked over at Angel, and she just shrugged her shoulders. When I looked at Netta, she did the same thing. *Damn, I guess me and Red both going crazy then.*

"Rae, what time should I be there for breakfast?"

"You can come about nine. We probably gon' start eating about ten."

"Well, I'ma show up at nine thirty then," G said and everybody laughed.

"That's fine by me, G."

Briscoe tapped me on the thigh. "Go get my baby, Rae, so we can go to the crib." Standing from his lap, I walked around the room one last time and said my goodbyes before going to grab a sleeping Saje from my dad. When valet pulled the truck around, I got in on the passenger's side while Briscoe strapped her in the car seat. Once he was done, he got in the driver's seat and pulled away from the restaurant.

"Tonight went better than I expected," I said through a yawn as I reclined my seat.

"It did, and I hope it stay that way. Everybody was kicking shit and getting along. Hell, even you and G was playing nice."

"Yeah. She liked me tonight, and that was odd, but I'll take it." I laughed.

"You gon' take this dick when we get home too, so don't even try to go to sleep."

"Um. I sholl am."

Briscoe was talking shit, per usual. His nightly routine was showering and sitting in the recliner with Saje. They would watch Coco Melon until she drifted off to sleep. Being that she had tapped out already, the moment his body hit the chair in the room, his ass was gon' be slumped. Briscoe reached over and grabbed my hand. Bringing it up to his mouth, he kissed the back of it.

"I love you, Rae baby."

"I love you too."

3

———

BRISCOE

"Oh shit... I thought you would be sleep by now," Rae said when she walked back into the bedroom and found me sitting at the edge of the bed stroking my dick.

"Um-hmm... Yo' ass thought you was gon' get out of giving me some pussy, but you thought wrong. Take yo' ass right back in there and take that damn muffin top of yo' head." Rae thought she was slick. When she got her ass out the shower, she put on one of them ugly ass dresses from Walmart and that damn bonnet.

Normally, I would fall asleep when I put the baby down, but I had snuck out of the restaurant to go smoke with the boys, so I was 'bout to wear that ass out.

"It's called a bonnet, fool."

"I know what the fuck it's called, just like I know what it

looks like. Come here, Rae. Quit playing and come put that pussy in my face."

"Baby. I'm tired." She pouted.

"I'm tired too. You ain't gotta do nothing but lay there." Rae walked out of the room and back into the bathroom. *I'm 'bout to get her ass.* Getting up from the bed, I followed her. Wrapping my arms around her waist from behind, I pressed up against her. "My dick hard as fuck, Rae, and you think I'm bout to let you go to bed."

"I've be—"

"We both been up all day. Give me five minutes, bae," I said, kissing her on the back of the neck. "I promise I'll be quick."

"Okay," she breathed out.

"Bend that ass over, Rae." She bent over the sink as I dropped to my knees and ran my hand up her thighs. "Open 'em." Her legs open, and I grabbed her ass, spread it apart, and buried my face in it. Rae's knees buckled when my tongue made contact with her clit, circling my tongue around it before sucking it into my mouth.

"Umm... this pussy taste so good, bae," I muttered, flickering my tongue against her clit.

"Baby," she moaned.

"Don't move, Rae." Using my hand, I stroked her clit while driving my tongue in and out of her.

"Oh God. I'm about to cum."

"Let it go then." Her body bucked back against my mouth as she rode the wave of her first orgasm.

Standing from the floor, I kicked her legs further apart and slid in. "Look at me, Rae." When her eyes found mine in the bathroom mirror, I winked at her and bit down on my bottom lip. I ground my hips into her as I stroked slowly. I promised I wouldn't take all night, so I was 'bout to make her feel me.

"You 'bout to get this pressure, and if you get loud and wake my baby up, I'ma make you pay for it."

"Okay," she whispered.

Stroking faster, I pummeled into her over and over while strumming my finger across her clit. Using my other hand, I spanked her on the ass. "Open your eyes and look at me, Rae."

"I can't," she whined and shook her head.

"Yeah you can. Throw that ass back." Thrusting her hips back, she let out light

whimpers. "Sssss... Um-hmm throw it back just like that, bae." I grabbed her braids and wrapped them around my hand, tugging slightly I pulled her head back. "Look at me, bae." Rae's eyes rolled back in her head before she opened them and tried to look up at me. "This my pussy, Rae."

"Yessss... Shit... Yessss. It's yours, baby."

"All mine?"

"All yours," she whimpered.

"You gon' cum for me, baby?"

"I'ma cum... Shit I'ma cum.

"Good girl... Cum, Rae," I growled as I erupted. Her body violently shook against me as she climaxed. "Damn, Rae..." My body twitched when I slid out of her. "I swear yo' pussy gets better every day."

"Nigga, let my damn hair go," She fussed.

"Oh shit. My bad." I laughed and released her braids. "You for me, Rae."

"I know, baby."

"Another round in the shower?"

"Let me check on the baby first," she said before walking out of the room.

I made love to Rae in the shower before carrying her to bed. After getting her situated, I went and got the baby from her crib. I fell asleep with Rae nestled under my arm and Saje laying on my chest. A nigga couldn't ask for a better way to end his night.

WHEN I WOKE UP, my girls weren't in the bed with me. Reaching over to the nightstand, I grabbed my phone and checked the time. It was almost nine in the morning, so I knew Rae had probably been up trying to make sure everything was straight for breakfast. Throwing my dreads up in a bun, I slid out of bed so I could get dressed and head downstairs.

"Look at this late ass nigga," Priest joked when I entered the dining room.

I flipped him off and spoke to everyone. Walking over to the table, I took my seat beside Rae and grabbed the baby out of her arms. "Why you ain't wake me up?" I asked, leaning over to kiss her on the cheek.

"Me and Saje tried. You wouldn't wake up. I was giving you some time. Your mama and Granny G running a little behind."

Before I could respond, I felt little hands on the side of my face. Saje was tugging at my beard. "My daddy," she said to Rae before burying her head into my chest.

"Little girl, he was my daddy before he was yours," Rae retorted, leaning over to peck me on the lip. Saje's bottom lip started to quiver as her eyes filled up with tears.

"Aww, Rae, you 'bout to make her cry," Mielle said.

"This lil' girl stole my man right from up under me," Rae added.

I kissed Saje the cheek and rubbed her back to calm her down. "Nawl, my baby just don't play 'bout me."

"Blessings is the same way with Priest. She only fool with me when he not around. That's why I'm glad I got Bishop," Mielle related. She and Priest had given birth to a baby girl a month before we had Saje. Being that they were born right behind each other, the two of them were joined at the hip.

"Blessings know her mama be getting on my damn nerves."

"The older they get, it'll change. It used to be like that with the twins, but now both of them be following up behind me. Noble be watching me trying to do everything that I do," Kross assured.

"I'm not so sure about this one," Rae retorted.

"Hey... Sorry for being so late," Netta said, walking into the dining room with G trailing behind her.

"Gramma!" Saje shrieked and reached for Netta. Once she was seated, I passed her off and threw my arms on the back of Rae's chair.

Rae stood from her chair and tapped a knife against her glass, garnering the attention of everyone in the room. "So now that everyone is here, we wanted to bring our family and close friends together to personally thank each of you for the continued support. We wouldn't be able to navigate through life as easily if it wasn't for y'all. Thank y'all for being a part of our village and helping us raise Saje."

When Rae started getting emotional, I gripped her hand and stood beside her. "Y'all know Rae don't deal well with emotions," I joked. "But seriously, what my baby is trying to say is thank you for all that you do. We appreciate that shit and y'all."

Rae wrapped her arm around my waist and leaned into me. "Now that I've gotten that out of the way, let's eat, y'all."

"You good, bae?" I asked Rae.

"I'm perfect." I nodded my head and leaned over to place a subtle kiss on her lips.

"My daddy!" Saje shouted, causing everyone to laugh.

———

After we finished breakfast, everyone sat around the table talking. Now that Saje had stopped acting funny with Rae, I was trying to sneak out of the room and go smoke.

"I don't know how y'all gon' be able to get away from that baby for a week." Rae's dad spoke up.

"I thought y'all decided to take her with y'all?" Netta queried.

"We are... I'm flying Veronica out with us so she can watch her while we go out."

"Why does she get to go?" G asked.

"'Cause I gotta work, and you barely wanted to fly to Atlanta for the baby shower," Ma Dukes answered for me.

"Y'all could've left that baby right here with us. We could've took turns watching her."

"Granny G, you know me and Rae don't let her spend the night away from us."

"And I wonder who's idea that was?" she retorted. *"Three."*

"Oh Lord. Here we go," Rae mumbled.

"Mine G... I feel more comfortable with my baby being in the same house as me when I close my eyes."

"So you say. Ever since you got with her, Scoota, you done changed."

"Hold on now… What you trying to say, Granny G?" Veronica interjected.

Granny G slammed her hand down on the table. "I said he changed when they got together. Scoota, you act like you ain't got no family. That girl is taking you away from everybody."

"Mama!"

"Granny G!" my mama and Red both shouted.

"Hush up, Kacen. Y'all don't wanna hear the truth."

"G…" I sighed dejectedly. "You and everybody else know that ain't true. I let y'all see and spend time with Saje all the time. Ain't nobody keeping her away from y'all. When Rae had the baby, I offered you a house; you would've been closer to us. You ain't wanna do it, so whatever this lil' issue is that you got with Rae you need to drop it. It's been going on for way too long. This shit between me and Rae is forever, G." I grabbed Rae's hand and squeezed it.

"House… The same house that you gave to her mama? Boy, what that girl done did to you? Yo' head so far up her ass that you can't see what she doing?"

"And what am I doing, Granny G? Please enlighten me."

"You robbing his ass blind. Scoota, I hope like hell you made her sign that prenup."

When G said the word *prenup*, I felt Rae's body stiffen up. I knew I had fucked up.

"Got damnit. I done sat around and listened to you talk shit 'bout my baby when all she done did was take yo' shit and try to get you to accept her. My baby don't need shit from yo' 'Scoota'. She got her own money."

"Veronica, I know she wrong, but you ain't gotta be disrespectful."

"Respectfully, Netta, fuck yo' mama with that nappy ass wig she got on."

"Oh no, bitch... You got the right one now," Ma Dukes stood up and charged at Rae's mama. Before she could reach her, Red jumped up and grabbed her.

"Come on, y'all. Don't do this," Kross said, trying to calm the tension down.

I dropped Rae's hand and stood up. "Everybody shut the fuck up!" I barked. "Have y'all forgot that my baby is sitting right there? G... I love you and I'll never disrespect you, but you wrong. Rae and Saje are my top priorities. They're my family, G. Baby, you gotta stop or you gon' push me away. Veronica and Ma, y'all are better than that. If y'all keep this bullshit up, ain't gon' be no fucking wedding. I'll take my girl and my baby and get the fuck on down. Play with it if ya want."

I tried to grab Rae's hand, but she snatched it away. I knew she was mad as fuck, and I would deal with the consequences when we were alone and not in front of the whole family. I leaned down and whispered sternly in her ear. "Don't show yo' ass, Rae. We gon' talk about it later." I kissed her forehead and walked out of the house.

"I LEFT the crib 'cause I ain't wanna be around nobody."

"Nigga, shut yo' ass up. You left 'cause you knew you had fucked up," Red said. When I left the house, I went to the bar to have a few drinks. I was trying to figure out how I was going to smooth this shit over with Rae.

"Man..." I drawled. "I did more than fucked up. Rae sent me a text and told me not to even bring my ass home tonight."

"Yeah, she was pretty upset after you walked out. The girls took her upstairs," Kross admitted.

"Upset ain't the word. Nigga, you better pray she still wanna marry yo' ass after the shit you pulled," Priest added.

"Bruh... Out of all the shit you could've listened to, you let G convince you to ask Rae for a prenup." Red shook his head and sighed. "Nigga what was you thinking?"

"I wasn't, and at the time the shit sounded valid. It was really a way for both of us to be careful."

"Careful for what? You love Rae, don't you?"

"Kross, man, you know I love that girl. Think about how long I chased her before she finally gave me a chance."

"So why the talk of a prenup?"

"'Cause the shit G was saying made sense. I got all of these properties and shit that I had before me and Rae got together. If we split up, do I really wanna have to part ways with some shit I built from the ground up."

"Bruh, you can't look at it like that," Red argued.

"Let me guess... Ain't neither one of y'all niggas got a prenup."

"Fuckkkk no..." Priest dragged out. "As much shit as I did to Mielle, I wouldn't be shit to try and make her sign a prenup. If she was to ever leave my ass, I'd give up everything I own. She got my kids dog."

"But what about your commercial building and the brewery. You would be okay with her getting those in a divorce settlement?"

"Again, nigga, she can have everything I got. Mielle ain't selfish, nor is she vindictive. If we was to ever split as long as I took care of the kids, she would be fine."

"Everything that I own was put in Boog's name the moment we got married. So shit, she ain't got nothing to take from me 'cause she own it all already."

"Yeah... I got A name on all of my shit too."

"Damn... So it's just me, huh?"

"Yeah, bruh, it's just you. A said Rae got your clothes packed, and they're waiting for you by the door."

"Rae know me well enough to know I ain't staying nowhere but in my crib with her and my baby. I'on play that shit."

"Nigga, you let her arch nemesis convince you to get a prenup, then she yelled it out in the room of close family and friends. Like I said, you better hope she still wanna marry yo' ass," Priest specified.

"Aye, did y'all see how fast this nigga's mama lunged at Rae's mama?" Kross said with a laugh. "On God, I cried when she called Granny G's wig nappy."

Rubbing my hands down my face, I chortled. "That would've been a funny ass fight. Ma Dukes from the hood. She got hands for days. But I ain't sleeping on Veronica either. She look like she could give Ma a run for her money."

"Meanwhile, G started all of this shit and sat back and watched it unfold. Like her ass was innocent. A lit into her something serious when you left. I ain't think she had it in her, but she really got G told."

"What you gon' do, my boy?" Priest asked.

Shrugging my shoulders, I sighed. "Fuck if I know. We gotta go to the venue tomorrow for our last walk-through. That shit gon' be awkward as fuck. Y'all know how Rae is when she mad. She get real reckless at the mouth. I'ma go buy her ass some flowers or some shit."

"Better get her ass some diamonds; fuck them flowers."

"I'll figure something out. Let's get a round of shots going on one of you niggas 'cause I'm in distress over here."

"I got the first round," Kross offered.

Pulling my phone out of my pocket I shot Rae a text message.

Me: Raegan, I'm sorry, baby

I watched the three dots dance on the screen for a few seconds before they disappeared. Rae was a prideful person, and if anything, I knew she was feeling embarrassed. That wasn't my intention, but I could admit that I should've kept it a buck with her about the prenup. I let G put a battery in my back instead of dreading that conversation. When I first brought up the idea of Rae moving to Miami with me, she had reservations, and I assured her that I would always have her, only for me to turn around and question her motives. I had to fix this before my girl took my baby and left my ass.

4

RAEGAN

When Briscoe left the house, the tension was so thick you could cut it with a knife. Netta and Angel tried apologizing on Granny G's behalf, but I honestly didn't wanna hear the shit. I get she was so-called looking out for her grandson, but what we had going on wasn't any of her business.

Briscoe knew how much his granny didn't fool with me, so why would he even entertain shit she was saying? My feelings were more hurt than anything because I asked him if the prenup was his idea or if someone had mentioned it to him. He looked me dead in the eyes and told a fucking lie. I was under the impression that our relationship was a lot stronger than that. Had he sat down with me and been genuine about the whole thing, I wouldn't have a reason to feel some type of way.

I never had to date a nigga for what was in his pockets because I was a self-made bitch and always had been. I let that love shit make me soft 'cause the old Rae would've whooped that nigga's ass for playing on my top like that. We're literally days away from walking down the aisle, and my mama and his mama almost came to blows. At the rate things were going, I didn't even know if the wedding was going to happen.

"Rae, are you okay?" Angel asked, peeking her head into my bedroom. After I was embarrassed in front of every-fuck-ing-body, I retreated to my room.

"I'm good, friend. You can come in." The door pushed opened, and in walked my girls with sympathetic looks on their face. "Y'all hoes get on my nerves." I chortled. "Why y'all look like somebody died."

"Bitch, we thought you was in here crying your eyes out or some shit," Mielle retorted.

Cocking my head to the side, I stared at her. "Y'all hoes know me better than that. Don't get me wrong, a bitch definitely in her feelings, but what the fuck I'ma cry for? That man let his bald-headed ass granny pump his head up."

"That was wrong on so many levels, Rae. I can't believe Granny G did that."

"I keep telling you, Angel, the Granny G that you know is completely different from the one that I've experienced. That old bitch ain't liked me since the day that she met me."

"Now I see how Priest felt when it came to the situation with him and my dad."

"I used to hear people say all the time that they couldn't be with someone that their family didn't like, and now I see why. I done had this man's baby, and her ass still don't fuck with me. How you claim you love my daughter but don't like her mama? Make it make sense."

"I don't know, Rae, but what you gon' do now? I mean, Veronica and Netta were about to fight."

"Girl, did y'all see the way Netta hopped up like she was 'bout to do something? Ma Dukes would've mopped the floor with her ass."

"Netta jumped up like she had something to prove. I cried when Veronica said something 'bout that wig."

"I know my daddy's wife think we some hood rats for real."

"Actually, she wanted to come in here herself to make sure that you were okay, but your dad told her that you needed time," Angel responded.

"Is he back yet?" I asked.

"No... Kross said they're at a bar. I told him that you had Briscoe's things packed and sitting by the door waiting on him."

"If only it was that easy. That man stubborn as hell. It'll be a cold day in hell before he let me put his ass out. But I'll tell you what I did do. I found an attorney, and when we sit down with Boss, she's going to be present. I'ma make his ass regret asking me for a damn prenup."

"Oh Lord Rae. Did you really?"

"Hell yeah I did, Angel. I hired Vanessa Vasquez, and she came highly recommended. I'ma eat his ass up in mediation." I reached out to a girl I used to dance with back in the day. She stopped dancing when she started dating a player from the Miami Heat. A few years back, they went through a nasty ass divorce, so she was able to refer me to her attorney.

"Why do I feel like this 'bout to get very messy?" Suny asked, shaking her head.

"Bitch, 'cause it is. You did the right thing, Rae," Mielle added.

"Who got my baby 'cause I sholl walked off and left her lil' ass."

"Your dad and his wife took her out back. Want me to go and get her?"

"Nope... She can spend the night with them."

"Oh, you being petty, petty," Mielle joked.

"I sure the fuck am. It's *fuck her daddy* right now."

"You just mad... It'll be different when he comes home."

"And won't. He texted me before y'all came in. I almost wrote back and spazzed, but I left him on read. Let's hit the town. I'm not 'bout to sit up in here while they out drinking. Matter fact, Suny, text Kross and ask him what bar they at. We 'bout to pull up on them."

"Yeah, that's that good bullshit. I'm here for it," Mielle teased.

I was 'bout to fuck my nigga's night all the way up. If I was in a funk, his ass was 'bout to be too.

—

After getting dressed, we left the house, heading to Blackbird Ordinary, the bar where the guys were. Kross was the only one that knew we were about to show up. The way I was dressed, you would've thought I was on the prowl. I had on the Versace mosaic print bralette with the pleated skirt to match, and the Medusa chain sandals. My appointment to get my hair done wasn't until the next day, so I had my braids thrown up in a high bun.

"Rae, don't go in here showing out," Angel pleaded.

"Girl, I'm not. Just wanna see that nigga drool for a lil' bit, then I'ma go home and get my baby."

"Yeah, we gon' see," Suny teased.

When we walked into the bar, I led them to the back where the pool tables sat because I knew that's where I would find them.

"Fuck y'all doing here?" Priest asked when he noticed us walking up.

"Boy, shut up. You know you're happy to see me," Mielle retorted, sliding her body in between him and the pool table.

Suny and Angel made their way up to their men while I decided to be petty and take a seat in the booth.

I was playing on the phone when I noticed Briscoe walking toward me. "So you ain't get my text message?" Briscoe asked, sliding in the booth beside me.

"Yep," I said putting emphasis on the p.

"Why you ain't text me back then?"

"Didn't think it deserved a response," I quipped, shrugging my shoulders.

Briscoe pinched the bridge of his nose, and I smirked. That was his signature move that he did right before he got mad. "Say, Rae, I know I fucked up, but I'm trying to make this shit right."

"Trying to make it right? Ha," I scoffed. "Making it right would've been you not letting Granny G gas yo' head up. Then you lied about it, to my face at that. If you wanna be single, just say that."

Gliding his tongue to the roof of his mouth, he rubbed the side of my neck before gripping it. "Quit. Fucking. Playing with me. Raegan," he whispered sternly against my ear, squeezing my neck tighter with every word. His mouth was so close that I could feel the heat discharging from his body.

A lone tear slid down my face when he let go of my neck. "Let that *single* word come out yo' mouth again and it's gone be me and you. I told you I fucked up, and I'm man enough to admit that shit. The shit happened, and I can't take it back. What you want me to do, Rae?"

"If you gotta ask, then don't worry about it," I mumbled, trying to keep it together. I was on the verge of breaking down, and the last thing I needed was somebody to feel bad for me.

Briscoe sighed and ran his hands down his face. "This ain't us, Rae. We don't do this arguing shit. We better than all of that."

"I used to think we were. Now I'm not so sure," I painfully admitted.

"You drove?" He looked off when I nodded my head. "Come on. Let's go home. I'ma get one of them niggas to drive yo' whip back to the crib. You gon' ride with me," he said, holding his hands out for my keys. He slid out of the booth and went and said something to Red.

"You gon' be okay Rae?" Angel asked.

"Eventually, I will."

"You know it's okay to be vulnerable. Let your guard down and tell him how you really feel," she whispered.

After saying our goodbyes, we left the bar hand in hand.

NOTHING WAS RESOLVED last night after we left the bar. We literally came home, picked the baby up, showered, and got in bed. The strange thing was we'd never had any real conflict in our relationship, so it was hard trying to navigate through the emotions.

Before we went to sleep, Briscoe let me know that he no longer wanted to do a prenup. I guess I should've been happy, but that was the furthest thing from the issue. Once he and Saje left the room, I called the attorneys office and cancelled the meet up for the following day. I realized the one thing that our relationship lacked was boundaries.

Since the beginning, Granny G had been able to give her input whenever she deemed it necessary. He'd never tried to correct her. Instead, he'd always laughed and swept the shit under the rug. The things he said to her the morning that shit hit the fan was the closest he'd ever gotten to putting her in her place. And believe it or not, I felt like that wasn't enough.

The disrespectful things that he'd allowed her to say and do, I would never. Wasn't nobody alive about to disrespect my nigga but me. After all of this time, I still didn't understand why she disliked me so much. We had a house full of people, and there we were at odds. I didn't plan on showing my face until it was time for us to leave for the salon. When Briscoe decided he needed a break from the baby, he would bring her to me.

I was scrolling through Instagram when the bedroom door swung open. I rolled my eyes at the sight of my fiancé. "Say, Rae... Get up, get dressed, and meet me downstairs."

"Why? I don't feel like being bothered right now."

"That wasn't a fucking question. It was a command. Get yo' ass up and bust a move. We 'bout to get this shit settled today."

"What shit?" I probed.

"Rae, just get up. Besides that, your daughter has been up all morning, and you been in here rolling around the bed."

"Fine!" I hissed, jumping from the bed. Briscoe stood in the doorway watching until I disappeared into the bathroom.

—

"What's this?" I asked, walking into the living room where my parents, Granny G, Netta, Red, and Angel were all sitting.

"Have a seat, Rae... We 'bout to have a family meeting," Briscoe said. My sister and my dad's wife were the only "family" members that were missing from this lil' powwow, so when I didn't see my baby, I assumed she was with one of them.

"So... What's up?" I asked, waiting on somebody to talk 'cause I didn't have shit to say.

"G... I'ma start with you. You was out of line the other day. Now I done let a lot of shit slide, but that ends today."

"Scoota, I ain't trying to hear none of that."

"Dammit, G... Let him finish speaking," Red spoke up.

"Like I was saying... G, that wasn't cool. Rae is Saje's mother, and you gotta respect that. On the strength of me she ain't never tried to keep her away from you, but with the way that you've been acting, if she decided that she ain't want you around her, I couldn't do nothing but respect it. The disrespect toward her is too much. Rae ain't did nothing to you for you to treat her the way you do. You took one look at her and ain't liked her since. Hell, you really ain't gave her a fair chance."

"'Cause she just appeared out of thin air. One minute, you was up there single, and the next, you moving back home and bringing a stray with you."

"Come on, G... You know it ain't even go down like that. Everybody can tell you that I chased Rae ass for a long time. She wouldn't give me the time of day. See, unlike you, the very first time that I laid eyes on her, I knew she would be my wife. I saw some shit in her that I'd never seen in anybody else. It took her a minute to realize it, but this shit between us was destiny."

"Y'all wasn't even together long enough for her to be moving across the state."

"G, she moved because I asked her to. She took a chance on me and did some shit that she was uncomfortable with."

"How you know she ain't after your money?"

"'Cause she don't ask me for shit. Rae came down here with a job lined up. She wasn't trying to live off me G. She wanted her own shit."

I listened to them go back and forth and tried to avoid rolling my eyes. G didn't like me 'cause she thought I was trying to replace her. That was the bigger issue. She acted like my nigga was her man.

"I'ma take the blame for how you act, G. 'Cause for a long time, it's been just you and me. When Meat died, I took on the task of being the man in the house, and yo' ass got spoiled. Rae ain't trying to take your place. I got enough love to pass around to all y'all. But loving me and Saje mean you gotta love Rae too 'cause she ain't going nowhere."

"Rae, I'm sorry. I can admit that I've been judging you without taking the time out to get to know you. When you and Scoota got together, he ain't come around as much. I took that as you keeping him away from me."

"Trust me, G, if that nigga ain't' coming around, it ain't because of me. Yo' grandson got attachment issues. Half the time, I be wanting his ass to leave the house, but he rather be up under me."

G tittered. "Well, Kacen calls me twice a day, and when he comes home, he makes sure to spend time with me. Scoota don't even take me to bingo no more."

"That's on me, and I'll make a conscious effort to do better, G."

"Well... that's all I ask for," she conceded.

"Now that we got that out the way, Veronica and Netta, both of y'all owe each other an apology. We family. We don't fight each other. I ain't saying shit gon' be perfect, but we should love each other enough to fight with our words and not our hands," Briscoe communicated.

Netta cleared her throat. "Ron, I'm sorry. I shouldn't have got mad at you for taking up for Rae."

"I'm sorry too, Netta. As much as G piss me off, I shouldn't have spoke on her wig. We good?"

"We good," Netta agreed. I was glad the two of them were able to make up. Since my mama had moved to Miami, the two of them ran the streets together. They were one in the same.

"Since somebody felt some type of way about us bringing Veronica on vacation with us, I'm willing to do a trial run with y'all." Briscoe ran his hands through his dreads and sighed. "We will leave the baby here while we go away *if* the three of y'all can handle it," he said, speaking directly to my mama, Granny G, and his mama. "Y'all can figure out a schedule and take turns keeping her overnight. Raemon, you and your wife would have to stay here in Miami until we got back if y'all want the same opportunity."

"You sure about this?" I probed.

"Not really. But I'ma try not to be so selfish with her," he muttered. I threw my hands up in surrender when everybody verbally gave in to his demands.

I was just thinking to myself that we hadn't set any boundaries, and Briscoe went out of his way to mend fences with the family. I was definitely feeling better than I had when I woke up that morning. I would accept Granny G's apology for now, but only time would tell if she really meant it. If that was the bulk of the issues that we had to come, then

I had faith that we would be okay. I loved Briscoe so much, and accepting his marriage proposal was also me accepting the craziness that came along with him.

Standing from the sofa, I motioned for Angel to get up as well. "I'ma leave y'all to it. Me and the girls got hair appointments that we can't miss. We shall see y'all later." Before I could walk out of the living room, Briscoe grabbed my arm.

Pulling me into him, he whispered in my ear, "You for me, Rae."

5

———

BRISCOE

In less than twenty-four hours, I would be a married man. A nigga was feeling all vindicated after I called the family meeting. I knew Rae was looking upside my head 'cause I hadn't stood up for her by putting G in her place. It took that shit at breakfast to happen for me to realize just how bad it was.

The night I brought Rae home from the bar, while we were laying in the bed, I told her that I didn't want the prenup. In reality, I'on think I ever really wanted it. I kind of just let my mind get ahead of my heart. That shit almost cost me my girl. Wasn't no way I was 'bout to be out here living without her.

"Nigga, you don't hear them calling yo' name?" Priest said, smacking me on the back of my head. We were at the wedding rehearsal, Rae wanted to get married at the former

Versace mansion, so I shelled out some fucking money to make it happen.

"Hell nawl. My mind was somewhere else."

"Better get it on this wedding 'cause Rae done turned into a whole bridezilla."

"Aww shit," I grunted, walking into the room where the ceremony was being held. Rae was standing in the center of the aisle going off on the Tanita, the wedding coordinator. "Raegan Henry... Fuck wrong with you?" I barked.

Mielle threw her hands up in the air. "Thank you, Jesus. Talk some sense into her 'cause she got one more time to holla at me, and she gon' be short a maid of honor."

Rae turned to me with tears in her eyes. "The florist got my order wrong, and because tomorrow is Valentine's Day, they can't find any black roses to go in my bouquets."

Wrapping my hand around her waist, I kissed her on the neck. "Calm down. I'm sure we can do something to try and fix it."

"I tried," Tanita objected. "There aren't any available within a fifty-mile radius."

"Shit, let's just spray-paint 'em then, Rae," I offered.

"Bae, it doesn't work that way," Rae pouted.

"And we can't use red because...."

"Their dresses are red. It won't look right."

"Okay... Tell me what you want me to do, Rae, baby."

"Nothing because it's too late. My day is ruined."

"Nonsense. How many you need and when you need them by?"

"The lady gotta make the bouquets tonight, and it was supposed to be two dozen."

"Bet. Give me her address," I stated, pulling my phone out of my pants to send a text. "She'll have them in a couple of hours," I said after I'd sent someone on a hunt for the roses.

"Now that that's taken care of, can we please start rehearsal?" Tanita queried. "The dinner is in exactly one hour, and I want to at least run through the ceremony three times."

"You gon' stop showing yo' ass, Rae?"

"Yes," she said, conceding. Walking off, I took a seat by my boys and waited on the coordinator to give us directions.

"Rae spoiled as fuck. I thought I had Boog ruined, but nigga, you got me beat."

"Nigga... Saje the exact same way, it's like they know I won't say no to their ass."

"I'm glad Angel simple just like me 'cause ain't no way I would be paying for all y'all niggas to stay here."

"If you think about it, I actually came out pretty good. Shit, y'all niggas my groomsmen, and y'all wives are the bridal party. In total I only rented out five rooms." Rae wanted the wedding party to stay at the mansion. She and Selah would be sharing her room since we couldn't see each other after the rehearsal dinner.

"Well, when you put it like that, I guess it ain't too much. But shit, Mielle would be sucking dick for a year if I dropped this much money."

"That iced-out timepiece on her wrist says differently," Kross argued.

"Early Valentine's gift, my boy."

"Fuck," I mumbled. "I forgot to get Rae something for Valentine's Day."

Waving his hand around animatedly, Priest said. "This wedding is all her ass would be getting out of me."

"I'm with Priest on that one," Red agreed.

"I gotta do something other than this for her."

"Yeah... Tell her ass *I do... and oh, by the way, Happy Valentine's Day*," Kross joked.

"I'ma figure something out before tomorrow."

"You ready for this bachelor party?" Priest asked.

"Nawl... If it wasn't for y'all niggas, I would be up in the room kicking it with Saje while her mama out doing hoe shit for the last time."

"But that ain't gon' happen. We 'bout to turn G5ive out."

My niggas bought a section at the strip club to celebrate my last night as a free man. My girl used to be a stripper, so that shit didn't excite me like it used to. I wasn't gon' tell them niggas that though. I was gon' let them live vicariously through me that last time.

"We ain't turning nothing out if we don't get this

rehearsal dinner over with. Where Rae find that lady from? She mean as fuck."

"Who the fuck knows. I know she costing me about as much as them high ass rooms y'all staying in tonight."

"Aye, Ms. Wedding Lady, can we speed this up? I'm trying to go see some ass and titties tonight," Priest's stupid ass said, making everybody but Mielle laugh.

"Tanita, don't pay my husband any attention. He's not himself when he's hungry," Mielle retorted. "Priest, sit yo' ass down and wait on her to call for you."

"Aite, Kid. Y'all better get a move on, or we gon' be winging this shit tomorrow."

"Nigga, this my wedding, not yours. Sit yo' impatient ass down," I heckled. Rae's ass was already on edge. I was trying to keep a low profile. Last thing I needed was her flying off the handle again.

***

"Girl, you gotta shake more ass than that if you trying to get my money," Kross fussed, frowning his face up at the stripper that was dancing in front of him. Baby girl barely had any ass to shake. I didn't know how she ended up in the section with us, but the way Kross was looking, she wouldn't be there too much longer.

"Yo' father-in-law look like he in love," Red said, causing me to look to the left at Raemon. Some big booty stripper was grinding in his lap, and the nigga had the nerve to have his arms around her waist.

"Hell yeah. 'Bout to give his whole lil' check away. He come back broke, his ole lady gon' beat his ass."

"You good though?" Priest asked.

"Yeah... Y'all niggas tryna get me fucked up."

"Just trying to show the man a good time."

Checking the time on my watch, I saw that I had a few hours to kick it with my boys before I left to go set up Rae Valentine's present. Just because tomorrow was our wedding day didn't get me an excuse to drop the ball. I arranged for some balloons and candy to be delivered to Saje. She was staying in the room with Selah and Rae tonight. But I was personally delivering Rae's.

"If it ain't the man with the master plan in the flesh," Red said, standing from him seat to dap Boss up.

"Fellas..." he acknowledged before taking a seat.

"Uh-uh... Lil' mama you gotta get up outta here with that slow twerking and shit. I had to beg my wife to let me out the house tonight, and this the type of dance I get?" Kross fumed, pushing the same stripper up from his lap and ushering her out of the section.

"Nigga, Suny must ain't break you off before you came here," Boss asked.

"Nawl, Boss. Man, that muthafucka got a lazy twerk. All that slow grinding and shit. That's what I got a wife for. I'm trying to see some cheeks clapping."

"Oh yeah, this nigga on one. Fuck y'all gave him?"

"This muthafucka over there done gave his ass a bean," I said, pointing at Priest.

"Dog, why you do yo' brother like that?"

"Shit..." Priest said, shrugging his shoulders. "Nigga said he wanted to have a good time. And don't go back and tell Mielle with yo' snitching ass. You barely in the crew and be running yo' mouth like a lil' girl."

"Nawl, nigga, that one was all on Blessings. I told yo' ass not to do it, but you don't want to listen to nobody."

"What he do?" Red asked.

"A couple of weeks ago, we was chilling at the crib, and Bishop wanted to race. Halfway through the race, he reached over and pushed the boy down. Blessings ran in the house and told Mielle so fast."

Boss and Priest's friendship was another one that had come full circle. Priest still fucked with him from time to time, but Boss was Blessings' godfather, and being that he didn't have kids of his own, he took his role very serious. That nigga represented everybody in the crew, and it wasn't a decision that we made without being advised by him. He knew all about our legal and illegal businesses.

"Man... Mielle wanted to beat my ass about that shit too. I still can't believe my baby girl sold me out." Priest faked hurt.

"Aye, pass me that bottle of 1942 so we can take a couple of shots. This nigga getting married in a few hours." Boss fixed shots and handed them to everybody.

Holding his glass in the air, Boss said, "To holy matrimony and all that other shit. Better you niggas than me."

"What kind of toast is that?" Priest asked.

"Nigga, just take the shot."

After taking the shot, Boss brought more strippers into the section. I had two asses in my face competing for my attention, but the only thing on my mind was getting to Rae. Pulling my phone out of my pocket, I shot her a text.

Me: WYA, Rae?

Rae Baby: Fountain Bleu.

Me: In fifteen minutes, I need you to slip out... It's gon' be a black Tahoe outside waiting on you.

Rae Baby: I can't leave my bachelorette party.

Me: You trust me?

Rae Baby: With my whole life.

Me: Good... Like I said, it's gon' be a black Tahoe sitting outside. Get in it. They gon' bring you to me. When you get to the mansion, I'm in the executive suite, top floor. Knock on the door and I'll let you in.

I watched the screen and waited for her to respond. My plan would only work if she agreed to meet up with me. When the three dots appeared on the screen, my heart skipped a beat.

Rae Baby: Okay, baby

If I timed it correctly, with traffic, it would take Rae thirty minutes to get back to the mansion. I was ten minutes away, so I would leave a few minutes after her.

I threw the two stacks that I had in my pocket before standing from the couch. "Thank you, niggas, for tonight, but I'm 'bout to slide. Got a pretty brown thing 'bout to pull up on me."

"Tell Rae we said hey," all of them said at the same time. I chuckled and walked out of the club.

I HEARD soft knocks on the door I looked around the room, making sure everything was in place before walking to the door. I stood behind the door when I opened it. Rae hesitantly walked in. Closing the door behind her, I admired her ass in the tight black jeans that she had on. "Damn, baby, you look good as fuck."

"Briscoe, what is this?" she asked, looking down at the rose petals on the floor.

"Follow the petals, bae," I advised. I walked behind her as she followed the path I had laid out. When she heard the music playing, she gasped and walked into the bedroom.

You never have to question the love I have for you
Girl I will put my life on bended knees for you
Ask all my friends, they'll tell you
You're all I talk about
Even when I go to sleep, you're the only one I dream about
See I'm your picture girl and baby you are my frame

And that's why I know our love will stay the same
So dry your weeping eyes
Girl I'm by your side
Just trust me I'm that guy
I'm in it for the long ride

I had "I'll Never Leave" by R. Kelly playing on the speaker, and her name was spelled out in candles on the table.

The moment her eyes landed on the setup, she stopped walking and turned to face me. "Bae!" she squealed, throwing her arms around my neck. I had lit candles, red balloons with one-hundred-dollar bills attached to the string, and red roses placed throughout the room. On the bed sat two orange Hermes boxes and three Chanel bags.

Nuzzling my face in her neck, I sniffed. "You smell good as fuck, bae. Happy Valentine's Day."

"Thank you," she sang. I tried to remove her arms from around my neck, but she shook her head and held on tighter.

"I know you not crying," I whispered into her neck. She shook her head, and I laughed 'cause I knew her ass was lying. "Come on, bae. You gotta let me give you the rest of your gifts."

"It's more?" she mumbled.

"Much more, girl." I tittered, peeling her body away from mine so I could give her the other part of her gift.

"Bae... You didn't have to do all of this," she whined when I handed her two Cartier boxes.

"Yeah I did 'cause I owe you an apology. I'm sorry for lying to you about something so simple. I ain't never had a reason to think you was with me for any other reason besides the fact that you love me. I'd give my last just to make you happy. I was wrong, and I'm man enough to admit that. You forgive me?"

"I forgave you when it happened. I know your heart, so I knew not to take that personal. I won't lie and say I wasn't hurt about you lying to me. We've always kept it real with each other, and when you feel like you gotta start lying to me, then I know we have a problem."

"Trust me, that shit won't happen again."

"I trust you."

"You ready for later on today?"

"Speaking of... Ain't it something like bad luck for us to see each other before the wedding."

"Ain't no bad luck over this way, baby. We on some forever type shit. Can't nothing come between this bond." Fixing two glasses of Ace, I handed her one and pulled a chocolate-covered strawberry out of the box. "Open your mouth," I ordered. I placed the strawberry in her mouth and watched as she bit into it. Using my tongue I caught the juice that ran down the side of her mouth.

I gripped her neck and brought her face to mine to kiss her. Her hand found my shirt as she bunched it up in her hand. Parting her lips with my tongue, I snaked it in and out of her mouth, causing a low moan to escape from her lips.

Setting the glass down on the counter, I used my free hand to unbutton her jeans. When I had them undone, I kneeled to the ground and worked them down her thighs. "Step out of them." I assisted her with stepping out of each leg, leaving her in only the lace bodysuit that she wore, and the pair of Giuseppe heels that were on her feet.

I ran my hands up her thighs until they reached her center. I gripped her ass cheeks and pulled her body into me, laying my head on her stomach. Her hands found their way to my head as she rubbed through my dreads.

"I love you so much, baby," I whispered into her stomach. Placing soft kisses on it, I kissed down her body until I was face-to-face with the thin black lace between her legs. Using my tongue, I swiped up and down the lace. Her body shuddered when I nibbled on her lips.

"The next time we make love, you'll be Mrs. McColister. But right now, I'm 'bout to eat the fuck out yo' pussy," I declared, using my hands to unsnap the body suit. Parting her lips with my tongue, I dove in face-first.

I circled my tongue around her clit as I grabbed her ass to hold her in place. Slightly biting down, I sucked her clit into my mouth flickering my tongue back and forth across it.

"Mmmm, bae," she moaned, bucking her body forward. "Damn, that feels good. Eat yo' pussy, baby," she uttered, rotating her hips to match my licks. Lapping my tongue up and down her slit, I sucked her lips into my mouth. "Oh shit, wait... Bae, wait a minute. I'm about to cum."

After her announcement, I flattened my tongue, running it up and down her slit before driving it inside her. "Cum. Give me all of that shit." My tongue was so deep off inside of her. I was trying to eat her insides out.

"Got damnit, Briscoe," she wailed as body violently shook. My hands rubbed her ass in a circular motion as I sucked on her pussy. Rae screamed out loud when her orgasm finally took over, causing her to squirt all over my face.

"Damn," I breathed out, licking her remnants off my mouth. "I think that's the first time you've ever did it like that."

EPILOGUE

Rae

I woke up to what sounded like someone pounding on the door. Jumping up, I searched the nightstand for my phone. When I couldn't find it, I flipped the covers back and slid out of bed. I grabbed a robe from the closet and put it on before going to answer the door. My eyes rolled instantly when I opened the door and there stood Kross, Priest, Red, and Boss.

"Why they fuck are y'all banging on the door so early?"

"Uh, excuse me, ma'am, we're supposed to be here. Yo' ass the one that supposed to be on the other side of the mansion with your girls," Priest said, pushing his way through the door.

"Ugh, I can't stand yo' ass. Wait 'til I tell Mielle you came in here with lipstick on your neck." Priest rubbed his neck and looked at his hands. "Oh, I'm definitely telling now 'cause if a bitch wasn't up on you, yo' ass wouldn't be rubbing like that."

"Fuck out of here, bruh. Wasn't no bitch up on me. I was just joking."

"Rae baby, I'm bout to order some breakfast what you wa—Fuck y'all doing in here?"

Holding up the bottle of 1942, Boss chortled. "Came to have shots with yo' ass since you dipped out on us last night, but you look a lil' preoccupied."

"Give us a few minutes, y'all." I laughed, grabbing Briscoe by the hand to drag him to the back of the suite. When we made it into the room, he picked me up and tossed me on the bed. "Baeeeee!" I squealed. "I gotta go so I can get dressed."

"Let me get that real quick," he begged, pulling at the strap of my robe.

"No... We can't."

"Why the fuck not?"

"'Cause them niggas out there and I gotta go to my room. We do have a wedding to make."

"I'ma be quick though."

"No," I asserted.

"Fine," he huffed, rising from the bed. "I'ma remember that shit when you ask for some head tonight."

"Um-hmm. That breakfast that you was 'bout to order,

can you get it sent to my room and order enough for the girls?"

"Aht aht. I'm broke, baby. I ain't got no money," he joked.

"Nigga, order us some breakfast. I'm 'bout to go. I'll see you later on." Tightening the robe around my waist, I threw my arms around his neck. "I love you. Thank you again for last night."

"I love you more, baby. I can't wait to make you my wife," he replied, leaning down to kiss me on the lips.

"I'ma suck that dick so good tonight," I retorted.

Briscoe laughed and smacked me on the ass. "Bye, Raegan."

"Bye, daddy," I called over my shoulder, walking out of the room.

———

"Oh, look at this bitch here doing the walk of shame," Mielle teased when I walked into the room.

"Lord, if it ain't them niggas, it's y'all. Selah, why you let them in here?" I said, rolling my eyes.

"Yo' ass better be glad them niggas showed up when they did. Knowing y'all asses, the damn wedding would've been delayed."

"Briscoe was already up." I walked into the bathroom and handled my hygiene before laying across the bed.

"Rae, you could've told somebody that you was leaving last night."

"My nigga called, and I had to go. Besides, y'all hoes was too busy watching dick to be worried 'bout me." When I left my bachelorette party last night, I didn't know what to expect. I was so surprised when I walked into the room. Briscoe really showed out. If that was the type of apology I would get, that nigga needed to show his ass more often.

"Uh-uh. Not me. I was sitting in the corner. That was Mielle and Suny."

"Shut up, Angel. Don't be repeating that. I told Priest we ain't have no stripper. I ain't trying to 'cause no problems."

I yawned and pulled the cover on top of me.

"Rae, the glam squad is here to get you ready," Selah said, peeking her head into the room door.

"About time. Get yo' ass up, Rae. We gotta start getting ready for this wedding," Suny ordered, snatching the cover down.

"Y'all, I'm really getting married today."

"Yes, bitch, you are."

"No, Mielle. Like I'm really about to be somebody's wife," I whispered with tears forming in my eyes.

"Oh my God, Rae. Why are you crying?"

"Because I'm happy," I sobbed. "I'm genuinely happy. I can't believe he wants to marry me."

"Of course he wants to marry you, Rae. You're smart as hell, and you're an excellent mom to Saje. Briscoe would be a fool to not marry you," Angel said, wiping tears from my face.

All of the prepping and planning that it took leading up to this day, and I still couldn't believe that I was about to get married. I'd never in a million years pictured myself being where I was. I actually had a baby and accepted someone's proposal. All of the bullshit that I went through led me right into the arms of my soul mate.

"Angel," I groaned. "What I tell you about all that damn crying?" I teased as I wiped her tears. "Whoo, okay. I'm ready. Y'all can let them in. Me and Saje gotta meet her daddy at the altar."

"Yassss. Say that shit, bitch. Somebody turn the music on and pop a bottle of champagne. Let me take this picture and post it with the hashtag #HappilyEverMcColister," Mielle shouted while twerking. "It's wedding time, bitches!"

Briscoe

"Nigga look casket sharp in that red blazer," Priest joked.

"You mad 'cause yo' ugly ass ain't look this good on your wedding day. Swole ass face was red 'cause you was high as fuck."

"Muthafucking right. I was nervous as hell. I had to take something to calm my damn nerves. Almost fucked my baby's day up."

"I don't know what you was nervous for," Kross added.

"Scared of being on locked down for the rest of my life shit."

"Marriage ain't nothing but logistics. Me and Rae been on some forever shit. The piece of paper just looks good for folks. This whole ceremony shit is for Rae 'cause she deserved that shit. I would've been okay riding out to Vegas or some shit. But I knew I had to go all out since she changed her whole life for me."

"Did y'all ever sort the prenup shit out?"

"Yeah. We ain't sign shit. I was riding down the block one day and I thought about some shit that Kross said."

"What I say?" he queried.

"When you said Suny was the realest on your team. That shit ain't resonate with me until I was thinking 'bout that prenup shit. Here I am scared that if me and Rae split, she gon' try and get my rental properties, but that shit wouldn't be what it is if it wasn't for her. The very first night that we fucked, I remember sitting out back by Priest's pool telling her that I needed a plan for when I hopped out the streets. She asked me what was I interested in, and when I said I thought about flipping houses, she said do that and then rent them out."

"See, that's that silent motivation."

"It really was, and every time I purchased a house to rehab, I did that shit with her in mind. All the shit I've done for her was because I wanted to, not because she asked."

"That's one thing that I appreciate about all of our

women; they can stand on their own without us," Kross added.

"Exactly, nigga. So shit, it wasn't no purpose in making her sign shit 'cause if her ass tried to leave me, I'd buy my way back to her heart." I chuckled.

"Not me. If Mielle wanna leave, I'ma help her pack them muthafucking bags. She can leave, but she gon' leave my chirren where they at."

"Cap!" Kross yelled. "Yo' big ass gon' cry if Mielle try and leave you."

"Shit, I'ma cry if Rae ass try to leave me." And that was the God honest truth. If my bitch ever packed her shit like she was gon' leave me, I'd probably have a nervous fucking breakdown.

"Briscoe, it's time," Tanita said, walking into the suite with a clipboard in her hand.

"Come on, my boy. It's time to go get you hitched.

—

"Damn. This don't even look like the same room," I said, peeking my head into the room where the ceremony was being held. When we did the rehearsal yesterday, the room was plain. Rae had already told me that they crew would be working early morning to set it up. The room was decorated so elegantly in a black-and-red color scheme. Long-stemmed red roses sat in black vases at the end of every aisle. Now I understood why she stressed that I wear a red blazer.

R. Kelly's "Forever" started playing as my groomsmen and I walked down the center of the room to take our place in front.

Hey Miss Beloved, we are gathered here
To join each other hand and hand
No more playing house, no
'Cause I want to make it real, do you understand?
To have and to hold (mm-hmm), until death do us part
No one, no one could ever interrupt the beats of our heart
'Cause this is gonna last...

WHEN WE LINED up beside Boss, who was the officiant, the doors swung open, and the girls walked down. My baby Saje was walking down with Selah, and when she spotted me, she ran in my direction. "Daddy!" she screamed, and everyone laughed. Rae had my baby dressed in a black floral lace type of dress. Scooping her up in my arms, I littered kisses on her cheeks.

"Saje, you can't be shouting and running off like that," I whispered. Selah tried to grab her, but Saje started whining. "She good. I got her."

The music cut to "Girl U for Me" by Silk when my angel appeared in the doorway.

> *Tonight is the night and the moon is right,*
> *Baby, let me tell you, I'm in love with you tonight.*
> *The more love we make and the more love we take,*
> *Let me tell you, I won't let you get away.*
> *Girl U for me, and girl me for U.*
> *I don't care what people might say.*
> *Just ask and I'll do, I'll do it for you.*
> *There'll be no more games that we'll play.*
> *The night that we met is the night I won't forget,*
> *How you touched my heart and you made me realize.*
> *I knew you were the one after all was said and done,*
> *Baby, can I tell you, that I want you by my side.*

"Only Rae could pull off a black wedding dress," I heard somebody say behind me.

I couldn't formulate the words to express how I was feeling right now. *God, she look beautiful.* I passed Saje back to Selah. I had to bend over and catch my breath. Watching her walk toward me brought tears to my eyes. When I stood up and looked at her, I saw that she was crying as well. When she reached me, I stepped in her space, ignoring her daddy.

"You look so fucking good right now, Rae," I mumbled, reaching my hand up to wipe her face.

"Baby, you're crying?" she asked using the back of her hand to wipe my tears.

"Hell yeah a nigga crying, I'm happy as hell right now."

"I'm happy too. Thank you, baby."

"What you thanking me for, Rae?"

"For showing me what true love felt like."

"I've loved you since the moment that I laid eyes on you. Thank you for giving me a chance to be that man for you, and thank you giving me Saje, my greatest gift ever. You for me, Rae."

"Forever."

"You ready to do this then?"

"I been ready."

The End